STAR TREK

What Would Captain Kirk Do?

by Brandon T. Snider

PSS!

PRICE STERN SLOAN

An Imprint of Penguin Random House

PRICE STERN SLOAN
Penguin Young Readers Group
An Imprint of Penguin Random House LLC

ISBN 978-0-399-53954-1   10 9 8 7 6 5 4 3 2 1

STAR TREK

What Would Captain Kirk Do?

by Brandon T. Snider

An opportunity to voyage beyond the stars is an enormous gift. The cosmos is filled with a great many wonders—uncharted worlds, bizarre life-forms, chaos, and calm. Tread carefully, and keep an open mind.

You never know what you might stumble across.

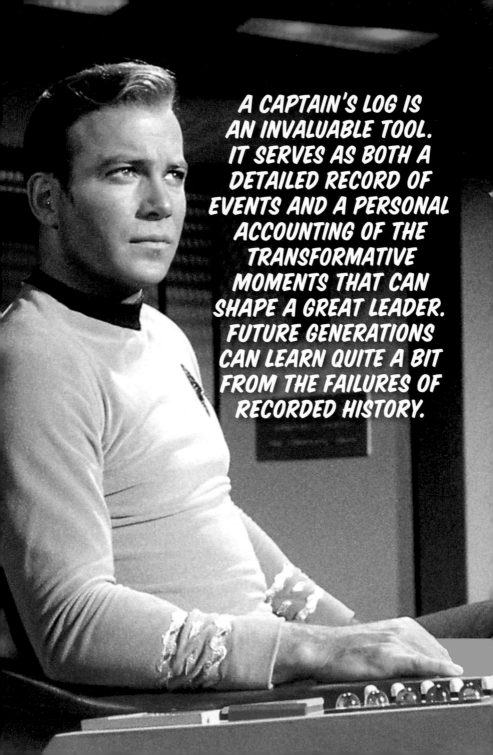

A CAPTAIN'S LOG IS AN INVALUABLE TOOL. IT SERVES AS BOTH A DETAILED RECORD OF EVENTS AND A PERSONAL ACCOUNTING OF THE TRANSFORMATIVE MOMENTS THAT CAN SHAPE A GREAT LEADER. FUTURE GENERATIONS CAN LEARN QUITE A BIT FROM THE FAILURES OF RECORDED HISTORY.

As you prepare for your journey into the unknown, assemble a crew of passionate yeomen and logical thinkers. A diversity of personalities is critical to maintaining balance. Trust is crucial to working together, but skepticism is a healthy attribute for a leader that doesn't want to get stabbed in the back.

The ability to outwit an opponent is an enviable one. You'll need to develop applicable strategies for a variety of situations and have them ready at a moment's notice.
A stern game face goes a long way.

It may even help confuse a Vulcan opponent during a particularly irritating game of chess.

Technology can be confusing, especially when an android takes the appearance of a beautiful woman, like Rayna.

As always, meet new situations with curiosity, a healthy bit of skepticism, and a defensive stance.

And don't judge an android by its cover.

The human mind is as advanced as any computer.

Grow its power with raw data and develop informed opinions. Protect it. And if control of your own mind should ever fall to a selfish machine bent on world domination? Fight back.

The human spirit is just as advanced as the human mind.

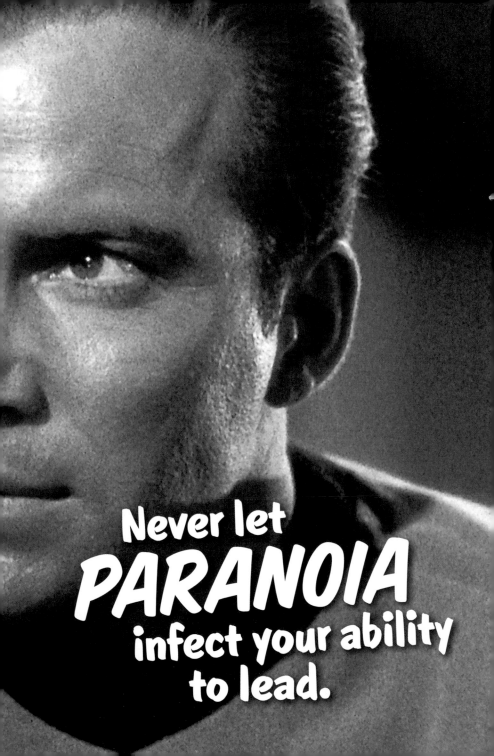
Never let **PARANOIA** infect your ability to lead.

THE UNIVERSE IS FILLED WITH MESMERIZING CREATURES. USE CAUTION WHEN YOU ENCOUNTER THEM.

Extend a kind hand to the **Alfa 177 canine** so it may sniff you. Once pacified, give the beast a gentle stroke to encourage it to drop its defenses. It may even yield to a light cuddle—that is, if a transporter accident hasn't already turned it into a feral doppelganger of itself.

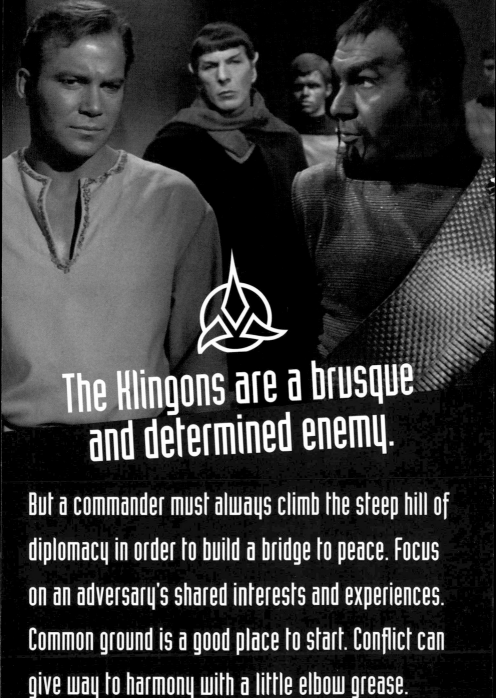

The Klingons are a brusque and determined enemy.

But a commander must always climb the steep hill of diplomacy in order to build a bridge to peace. Focus on an adversary's shared interests and experiences. Common ground is a good place to start. Conflict can give way to harmony with a little elbow grease.

THE HUMAN PSYCHE IS CAPABLE OF GREAT DELUSION. ONE MUST SIFT THROUGH ITS MANY LAYERS IN ORDER TO REVEAL AN EXISTENTIAL TRUTH.

Though the rigors of leadership leave little time for frivolity, humor is an essential component of being a versatile captain. Self-deprecation should be used well and sparingly. A crew should feel comforted by their captain's wit and charm. A smile can be a leader's best defense against monotony.

Don't just be a leader, be a friend.

Dabbling in the occult is a treacherous thing. It can easily enthrall an idle, impressionable mind.

If your starship is cursed, however, you may need to rely on your mystic friends. So keep an open mind.

When confronted with accusations of negligence against one of your crew members, compile all relevant facts. Interview all connected parties, and then conduct an intense and thorough investigation.

Never underestimate a threat from within. A petty man's jealousy can be just as dangerous as the most implacable Romulan or Klingon foe.

A commander must consider every appeal for assistance, no matter its origin. Assess requests thoroughly before acting to avoid clear and present danger.

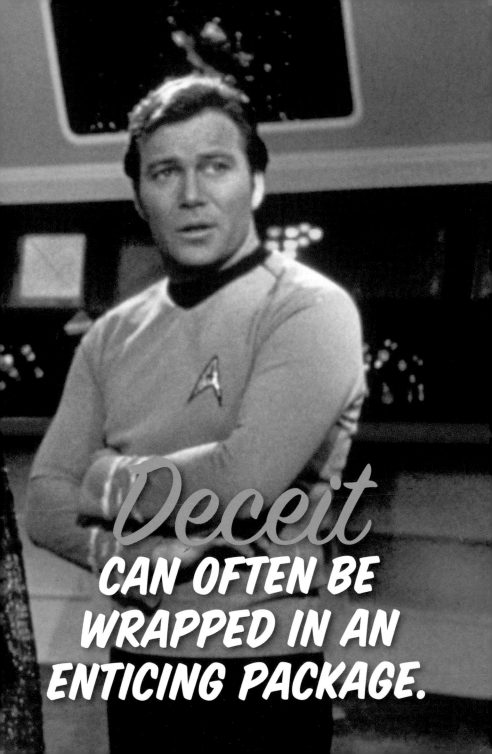

Deceit CAN OFTEN BE WRAPPED IN AN ENTICING PACKAGE.

When in doubt,

set
phasers
to stun.

When in ROME...

As you travel through space, it's sometimes vital to conceal your identity and take on the customs and clothing of other cultures. By fitting in, you will gain the trust of your new friends and see the world through completely different eyes.

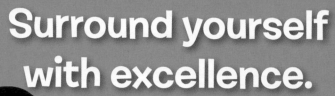

Surround yourself with excellence.

Don't be afraid to let your colleagues each have their moment to shine.

Envious leaders select an inept crew to make themselves feel superior, but great leaders embrace those they can learn from and push them to great heights.

Have patience when a hostile Kelvan transforms your colleagues into porous cuboctahedron solids. Though it may be frustrating, take note of your enemy's concerns before acting in haste. One false move and your companions might be crushed into oblivion with relative ease.

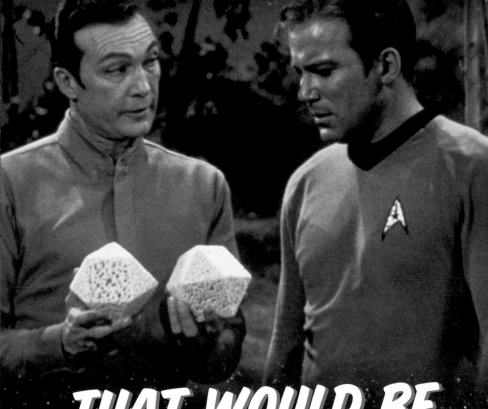

THAT WOULD BE A BAD THING.

Should you ever encounter a sentient gateway through which one can travel beyond time and space, remain even-tempered. An entity with that much power is bound to be perplexing. Treat it with caution and respect, even if it responds with arrogance. You need not make an enemy.

THERE ARE ALWAYS
CONSEQUENCES TO
TIME TRAVEL.
Always.

Psychiatric self-experimentation is ill-advised, especially if you oversee a galactic penal colony. Why complicate a situation already wrought with madness? If you have access to a Vulcan mind-meld, use it to help expedite the healing process. If you don't have access to a Vulcan mind-meld, good luck.

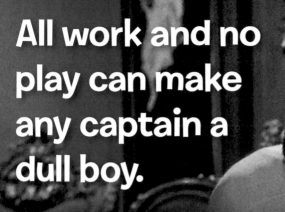

All work and no play can make any captain a dull boy.

Always take time for extracurricular activities. A relaxing game of billiards will help alleviate stress when the pressures of command weigh heavy upon your breast. A little bit of fun can often go a very long way.

WHEN ABRAHAM LINCOLN ASKS TO BEAM ABOARD YOUR SHIP, ACCOMMODATE HIM. HE'S A WISE MAN.

JUST MAKE SURE HE'S NOT A FACADE CREATED BY A SHAPE-SHIFTING ROCK CREATURE THAT USES MIMICRY FOR SPORT.

A STRONG LEADER KNOWS HOW TO FIND THE LIGHT.

Command is wrought with anxiety. Take caution not to panic. Breathe deeply and, if you find yourself in need of council, turn to a trusted crew member for advice.

Explain your situation clearly, making sure you don't shake your colleague into a seizure.

Never
let a
good
thing

slip
through
your
fingers.

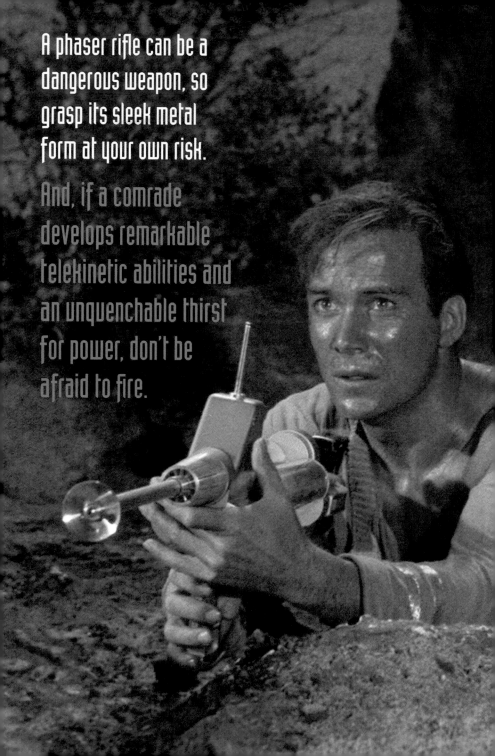

A phaser rifle can be a dangerous weapon, so grasp its sleek metal form at your own risk.

And, if a comrade develops remarkable telekinetic abilities and an unquenchable thirst for power, don't be afraid to fire.

The element of surprise can be a captain's greatest asset. Use it wisely.

PREDICTABILITY IS OVERRATED.

Your colleagues are watching you.

Be on your best behavior.

ALL STARFLEET OFFICERS MUST SUFFER.

If they don't, how will they ever
find out who they truly are?

If you find an ally has become consumed by the mating rituals of his homeworld, don't panic. Irrationality and illogical thinking can occur during such a rite of passage. Try using a simple deception to jolt your comrade out of his carnal haze.

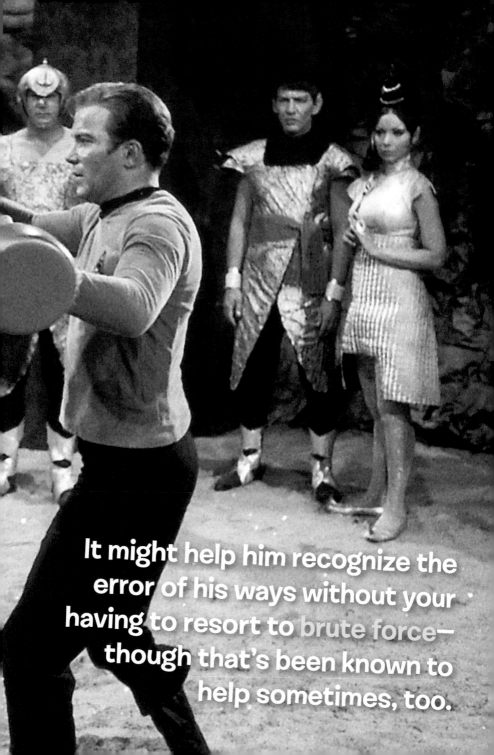

It might help him recognize the error of his ways without your having to resort to brute force—though that's been known to help sometimes, too.

When hand-to-hand combat isn't enough, one must turn to something colder and more effective. The use of lethal weaponry is a serious matter and should be treated as such. Don't let fear cause you to act carelessly.

LIFE IS FAR TOO PRECIOUS, EVEN WHEN IT BELONGS TO THE ENEMY.

Knowing yourself is an integral part of being a leader. Should a transporter malfunction ever split you into two separate beings, each with a distinct emotional disposition, only you will be able to navigate the more challenging aspects of your personality.

There's a time and place for impish behavior.

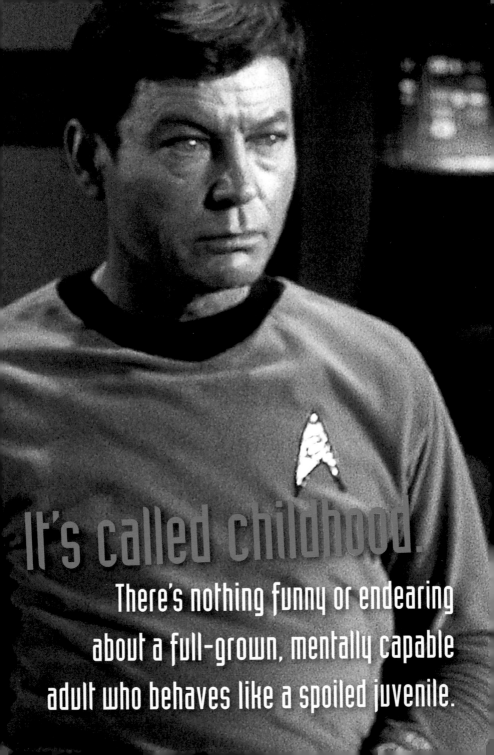

It's called childhood.

There's nothing funny or endearing about a full-grown, mentally capable adult who behaves like a spoiled juvenile.

A UNITED FRONT MAKES A STRONG STATEMENT TO YOUR ENEMIES.

Tread carefully when negotiating a disagreement on another planet. Acknowledge territorial claims and listen to both sides. Peace may often be hard-won, but it's always worth the struggle. Someone may even name an infant monarch after you.

That's always flattering.

THE RELATIONSHIP BETWEEN GOD AND MAN IS A COMPLICATED ONE. CAN MAN BUILD A BRIDGE TO HEAVEN? IT'S A QUESTION HUMANITY HAS ASKED ITSELF FOR CENTURIES. IF YOU AND YOUR CREW DISCOVER A PARADISE FILLED WITH UNENDING DANGER, PERHAPS IT'S NOT HEAVEN AFTER ALL. BUT THE QUESTION THEN BECOMES . . . WHAT IS IT?

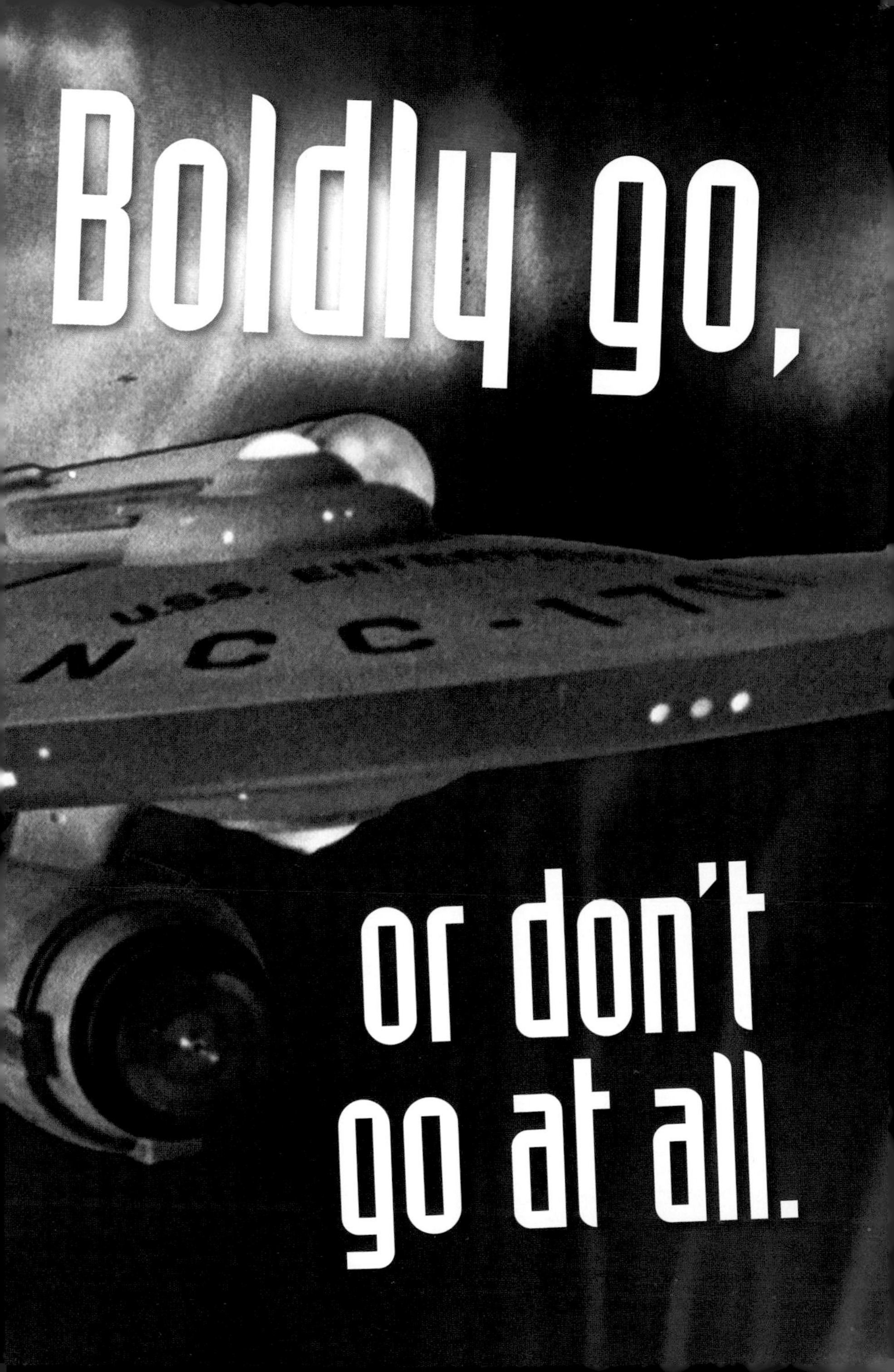
Boldly go,
or don't
go at all.

Have you ever been captured and forced to compete in gladiatorial combat just to delight your disembodied alien jailers? It's a tough spot to be in, but it happens to the best.

Gamble on your better instincts and take a risk.

What do you have to lose?

Every human being has the ability to control his or her own destiny.

No one is a prisoner of time.

The future has yet to be written.

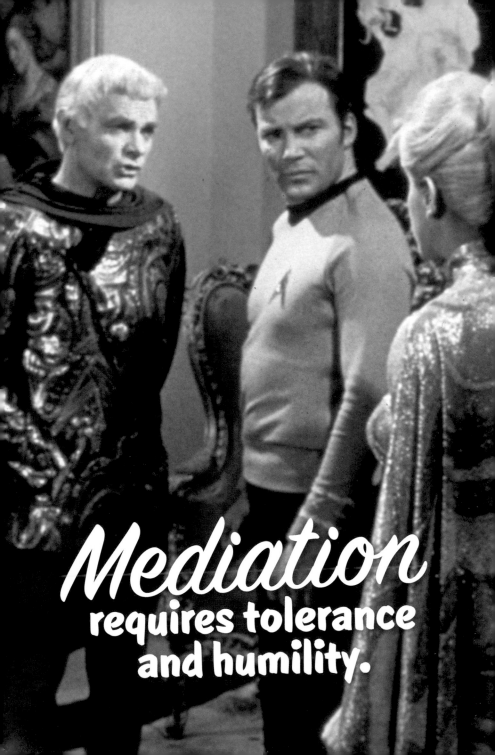

Mediation requires tolerance and humility.

Many of life's deeper truths are revealed when inhibitions are shed. The shedding of inhibitions is quite an experience, both pleasing and frightening. Especially when you are confronted with your own passions.

Acknowledge your feelings and, when the harsh light of reality arrives again, recalibrate your path

TIME IN
CAPTIVITY IS
BEST SPENT
PONDERING
LIFE'S
MYSTERIES AND
CONUNDRUMS.

Computer simulations
can be incredibly lifelike.
Don't be easily fooled.
If you find yourself in
conflict with a virtual
reality, offer peace
as an alternative.

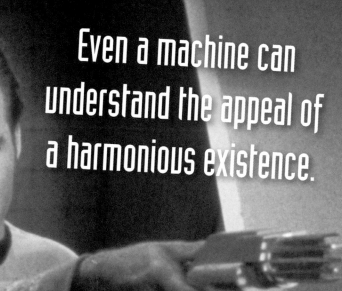

Even a machine can understand the appeal of a harmonious existence.

Social gatherings are the perfect time to mingle with the galaxy's most curious species.

The porcine Tellarites, for instance, enjoy the heated exchange of ideas— and not just because they have a naturally warmer body temperature.

Prejudice

is an awful disease.

Walk in the shoes of your enemy before casting aspersions, and when you see an adversary in distress, help them. Be the better person. It's the right thing to do.

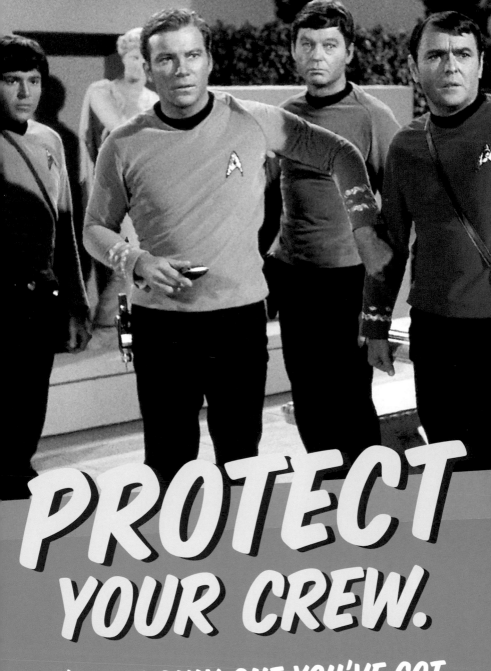

PROTECT
YOUR CREW.
IT'S THE ONLY ONE YOU'VE GOT.

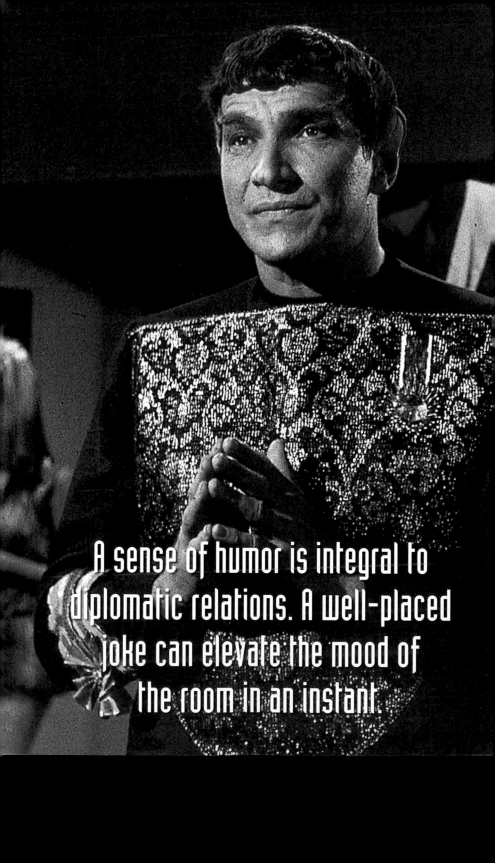

A sense of humor is integral to diplomatic relations. A well-placed joke can elevate the mood of the room in an instant.

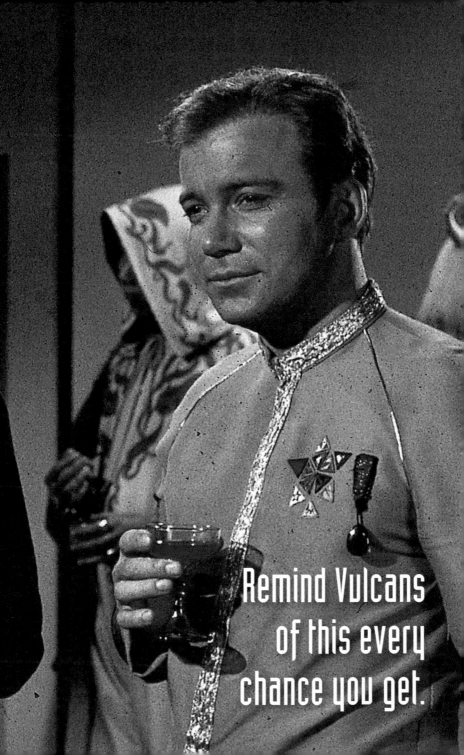

Remind Vulcans of this every chance you get.

The cosmos is filled with believers. Even Plato has apostles beyond the stars. Should you find yourself in direct conflict with these devotees, be respectful but determined.

And never confuse faith with sadism.

Technological advances can be
overwhelming, especially when
a machine reprograms itself
to sterilize the human beings
it perceives as imperfect.

Does perfection exist? Perhaps.

In the meantime, use logic, reason, and mild
trickery to disable the errant probe gone mad.

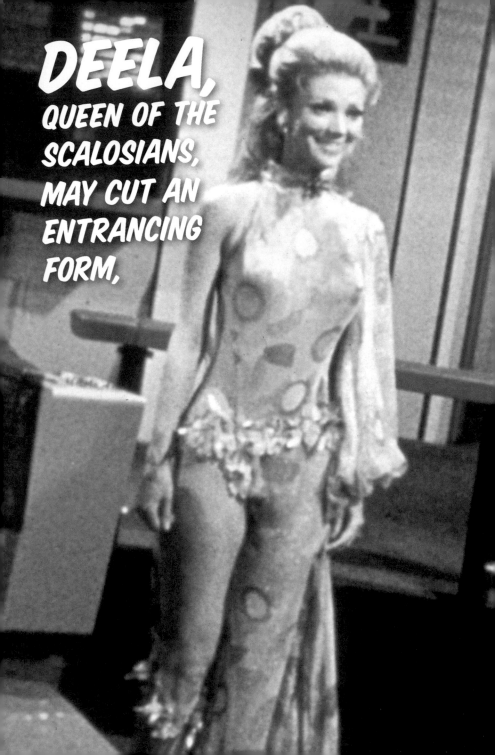

DEELA, QUEEN OF THE SCALOSIANS, MAY CUT AN ENTRANCING FORM,

BUT MAKE NO MISTAKE,
SHE ONLY DESIRES YOU FOR
BREEDING.

A captain cannot make up
his own rules. He's got to
do things by the book.

History is a fragile thing.

Live in the moment, take nothing for granted, and give freely of yourself.

You never know when your timeline might shift.

Lieutenant Nyota Uhura:

Her name means freedom, and she's the epitome of class, beauty and professionalism—and a fierce warrior to boot. If you're ever thrown together with someone on a bizarre world and forced to play out passionate scenes for the enjoyment of your alien captors, you should hope it's with her.

Travel space for millennia, chart countless worlds, battle evil in its darkest hiding places, and you won't find a better brother in arms than Spock.

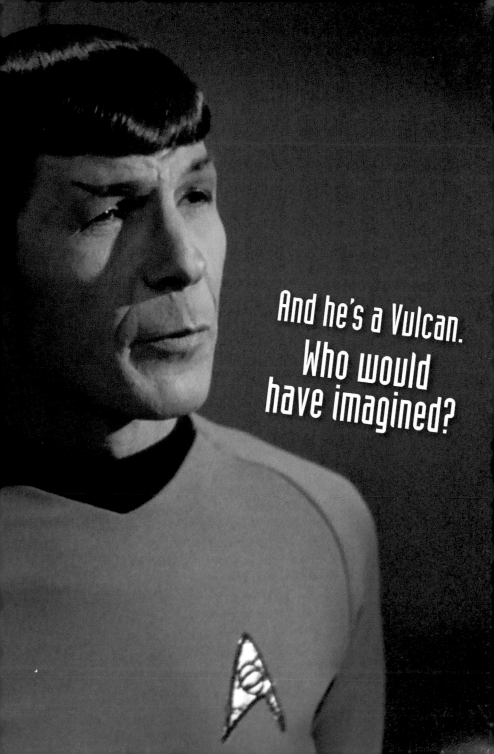

FRIENDSHIP
IS A GIFT TO BE
CHERISHED FOREVER.

SURROUND YOURSELF WITH FRIENDS, AND YOU'LL NEVER BE ALONE.

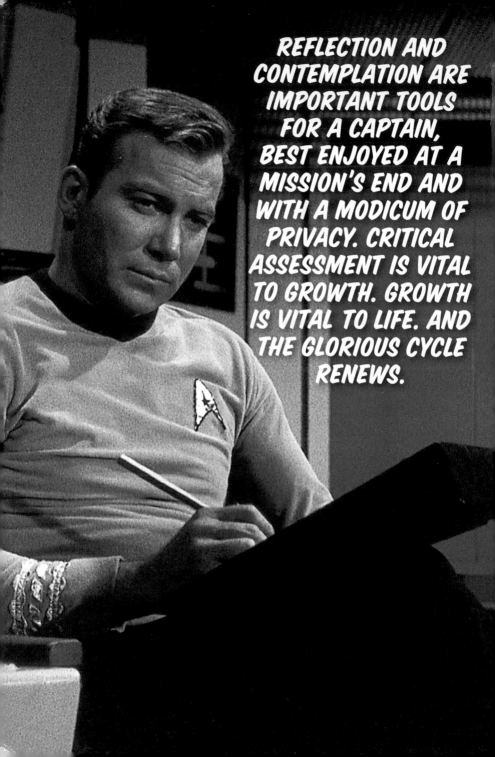

REFLECTION AND CONTEMPLATION ARE IMPORTANT TOOLS FOR A CAPTAIN, BEST ENJOYED AT A MISSION'S END AND WITH A MODICUM OF PRIVACY. CRITICAL ASSESSMENT IS VITAL TO GROWTH. GROWTH IS VITAL TO LIFE. AND THE GLORIOUS CYCLE RENEWS.